Milly and Molly

For my grandchildren
Thomas, Harry, Ella and Madeleine

Part of the proceeds from the sale of this book go to 'The Friends of Milly, Molly Inc., a charity which aims to promote the acceptance of diversity and the learning of life skills through literacy - *'for every child, a book.'*

Milly, Molly and Different Dads

Copyright © MM House Publishing, 2002

Gill Pittar and Cris Morrell assert the moral right to be recognised as the author and illustrator of this work.

Published by
MM House Publishing
P O Box 539
Gisborne, New Zealand
email: books@millymolly.com

Printed by Rhythm Consolidated Berhad, Malaysia

ISBN: 1-86972-021-0

10   9   8   7   6   5   4   3   2   1

Milly, Molly
and
Different Dads

"We may look different
but we feel the same."

It was a cold, wet, winter morning.
Miss Blythe asked everyone to take off
their wet shoes and put them by the heater.

"Come on, let's get warm," she said,
rubbing her hands firmly together.

No one had missed Sophie until, slowly,
the door opened.

Sophie stood dripping. It was hard to tell whether her face was wet with tears or raindrops.

"Come here, Sophie," Miss Blythe said gently.
"Let's take off your wet coat and shoes."

"Can you tell us what's happened?"

"Dad packed his suitcase and left home,"
sobbed Sophie.

Miss Blythe held Sophie against her
warm cardigan and said softly,
"Let's talk about our dads."

"My dad's in the hospital," started Jack.

"I've got two dads," said Elizabeth.

"I've only got one dad," said Milly.

"My dad's away with the Army and I only see him sometimes," Harry added.

"My dad's at home every day," slipped in Tom.

"I go and stay with dad for holidays because he has another family now," said Poppy.

"My dad's in a wheelchair," stated Humphrey.

"Dad adopted me when I was one," said Molly.

"Uncle Stan looks after me like a dad,"
added George thoughtfully.

"My dad is blind," said Meg.

"Dad died last year," Alf said quietly.

"And my dad died when I was six,"
confided Miss Blythe.

Sophie squeezed in between Milly and Molly.

"My dad is deaf," she said softly.

"So there we are," Miss Blythe said.
"All dads and families are different.
That's just the way it is."

Milly, Molly and Different Dads

The value implicitly expressed in this story is 'acceptance of family diversity' - to understand and accept that all families are different.

Miss Blythe encourages the class to share their dads differences to help Sophie accept that all families are different when her dad leaves home.

"We may look different but we feel the same."

MM House

PUBLISHING

Other picture books in the Milly, Molly series include:

- Milly, Molly and Betelgeuse   ISBN 1-86972-011-3

- Milly, Molly and Jimmy's Seeds   ISBN 1-86972-007-5

- Milly, Molly and Oink   ISBN 1-86972-009-1

- Milly, Molly and Pet Day   ISBN 1-86972-010-5

- Milly, Molly and Taffy Bogle   ISBN 1-86972-008-3

- Milly, Molly and the Tree Hut   ISBN 1-86972-013-X

- Milly, Molly and Beefy   ISBN 1-86972-012-1

- Milly and Molly Go Camping   ISBN 1-86972-025-3

- Milly, Molly and Aunt Maude   ISBN 1-86972-033-4

- Milly, Molly and the Sunhat   ISBN 1-86972-032-6

- Milly, Molly and Alf   ISBN 1-86972-022-9